Thunder's Hair

Jessie Taken Alive-Rencountre

Illustrations by Erin Walker-Jensen

Award Winning Author

Thunder's Hair

1st printing. Printed in 2020

For more information, please contact:
Jessie Rencountre
www.jessie.rencountre.com
jrencountre@gmail.com

ISBN: 9798560343996

Printed in the United States

Many Indigenous Cultures in North America have known for thousands of years that our hair is sacred. The many teachings share that when we wear our hair long it helps with the connection to the spirit world and helps guide us when we walk in life.

For thousands of years, women, men, and children would grow their hair long and wear it in braids.

This teaching, along with other cultural teachings, was almost lost when Indigenous children were forced to boarding schools and stripped of their cultural identity, one being the cutting of their hair short.

Many families are returning to the traditional teachings and honoring their children by letting their hair grow long.

Because there is a lack of education about this powerful and beautiful teaching of hair, many boys and young men have been victims of bullying.

This book is meant to empower our young boys to take pride in who they are as well as educate their peers and others why Indigenous people consider our hair sacred.

The sun was rising with a beautiful pink glow and begin to show life to the East. Thunder's mom set his stool facing the window to the east just like she did every morning. It was their morning ritual that started their day. She combed Thunder's hair and quietly sang a morning song as Thunder sat rubbing his eyes to wake up. "Son, what are your hopes for the day?"

Thunder yawned, "I hope that I pass my spelling test and kids are nice to me."

Thunder's mom continued to braid and said, "What do you mean, you hope they are nice?"

Thunder sighed, "Oh, just sometimes they can say things that upset me."

Thunder's mom grew quiet as she watched the sun light up the sky. She said, "Sometimes when others are mean, it's because they are hurting inside and forget who they are when they were born. Just smile at them and walk away. If it continues you can always get help from a teacher. Continue to lead by example and show others how to be kind."

His mom continued to braid his hair, placing the three strands, one over the other and sliding over her fingers. It always seemed like she was putting her wishes into each strand as she gently braided. When she was done, she put the elastic at the bottom of the braid and kissed him on the forehead. She said, "Son, I hope you have a great day today. Don't forget to ask for good things and wisdom when you leave the house."

The morning went by quickly and Thunder's spelling test wasn't so bad after all. The morning recess bell rang, and he welcomed the fresh air as he walked out to the courtyard. Just then he saw two boys running towards him. "Hey Thunder, where's your dress? Only girls have long hair!" Both boys laughed as one of the boys started to dance around and pretend to sing a powwow song as he hit his hand against his mouth, portraying an old "Hollywood Indian."

Thunder shook his head in disbelief and walked the other way. Just then one of the boys came running behind him and pulled on his hair. He snarled and said, "You know, I can give you a haircut when we get back inside. I'll help you understand what it is like to be a boy and live in today's world."

Thunder felt his face getting hot and clenched his fists. He was just about to push the other kid when he remembered the words of his grandpa, "We become the lesser version of ourselves when we solve our problems with our fists." Instead, he took a deep breath and pulled his long braid into his sweater and turned away.

Keya came running quickly. She hollered, "Hey, leave him alone! Quit being a bully!"

The boys ran away laughing as if they had accomplished something big. Keya glared at them as they ran away and said, "Yeah, keep running, you big bullies!" She turned her attention to Thunder and quietly asked, "Are you ok? You know, it's ok to tell the teacher and let her know what they say."

Thunder shook his head and said, "No, they'll think I'm tattling."

Keya said, "There's a difference between reporting something when someone is being hurtful to another compared to tattling just to get someone in trouble. If you let them go, they will continue to say things to you and even pick on others. If you won't tell, I will."

Keya must have kept her promise because by the afternoon Thunder was sitting in the principal's office being questioned about the incident that morning. Even though he did not want to tell, he shared as many bullying events as he could remember.

The car ride home that day seemed a long and quiet one as his mom's eyes swelled with tears. "I wish you would have told me about the disrespectful remarks of your long hair earlier, son. We could have put a stop to this when it started happening."

Thunder looked out the window, watching the trees and houses pass by. He sighed and mumbled, "What's the use? If we get them to stop, it will be another kid next year. It's just best that I cut my hair, so nobody has anything to say. My life would be so much easier with short hair."

When they pulled into the driveway, Thunder grabbed his backpack and walked toward the front door. His head hung low, feeling hopeless, and defeated. He turned to look at his mom and saw her wiping her tears. "This has caused me a lot of pain, and now you too. If you will not cut my braid, I will cut it off myself this evening," Thunder said sadly.

He threw himself on his bed and stared at his posters hanging on the wall. "All of these superheroes have short hair. None of them have long hair or look like me", he thought.

Just then there was a knock on his bedroom door. His grandma peeked in with her usual gentle smile, "Grandson, will you help me carry the wood for the sweat lodge?" Thunder would never tell his grandmother no, so he happily went out to help.

As he carried and placed the logs just right in the fireplace grandma asked him to join her as she watched and listened to the crackling fire.

 "Our ceremonies have been around for many years now, grandson. They have helped our people through so many hardships. I have seen a lot of changes over the years since I was a young girl many years ago. My grandma would tell me about what it meant to be a warrior. She said that a warrior is not someone who just protects other people, they also protect their own spirit. When others try to make us feel bad for who we are, warriors stand strong and proud, continuing to be who they were born to be."

Grandma took her hair clip out of her silver hair, let it out and started to braid it. "Our people have always known the power of our hair. These teachings have been passed down for thousands of years. We say that our hair has a special part of us in it, our spirit. It is our connection to the ancestors before us and to the spirit world. When we wear it long it helps us in this physical world that can be confusing at times." Grandma continued to braid her hair. She said, "Each of these three parts represent the three parts of us, our mind, body, and spirit. This is why we take care of our hair and why our people continue to wear our hair long. If we cut it, we lose that special connection."

Thunder suddenly felt a sense of pride in his long braid as he stared into the fire. He could not believe he had thoughts of cutting his hair earlier. He knew exactly what he wanted to do.

The next morning, Thunder asked his mom to braid his hair into two braids. He closed his eyes and envisioned past warriors with their hair in braids and paint on their face. He also imagined his strong lawyer uncle and his long braids.

When it was time to walk into school, Thunder walked with a sense of pride, like a modern-day warrior. He knew that he carried with him the strength of warriors of the past and today. As he walked, he saw the two boys and could hear the whispers and even giggles around them. This time, he did not hang his head. Rather, he walked proudly over to the boys and said, "I was born with this brown skin. This is who I was meant to be. I am proud of who I am because I carry the strength of many warriors with me. You will *never* make me feel bad for who I am and how I choose to wear my hair. There is strength in accepting others who are different than us. I hope that someday you will learn this too."

Thunder turned away and started walking toward the door of the school. He could imagine the sound of the drum beat in his head as he stepped with confidence. Each stride he took made him imagine past warriors walking where his feet touched the ground. He stood tall and smiled as he saw his reflection in the window of a young warrior staring back at him.

Special thanks to:

Tyler and Thunder

Tusweca, Wiconi, and Omaka

About the Author

Jessie is a Hunkpapa Lakota from the Standing Rock Sioux Tribe. She grew up around her culture and has been influenced by Lakota values passed down to her from her parents and grandparents. She has spent the majority of her career working as a school counselor with elementary and high school students. She is the mother to Jaylee, Sophia Sadie, and Mila. Her experience of working with children, being a mother, and growing up around her Lakota culture have been big inspirations for her to write books for children. Jessie and her husband Whitney make their home with their daughters in the Black Hills of South Dakota.

About the Illustrator

Erin Walker-Jensen, a cousin to the author, is an artist from Fort Yates, ND. She grew up on a farm on the Standing Rock Reservation. Erin has been creating artwork since she was a youngchild. She resides in Mandan, ND with her husband and children.

Made in the USA
Middletown, DE
27 September 2023

39302864R00022